M

Happy First Mothers Day.
You and Benjamin
are heavenly made -
I see it everyday.

Love ♡

Heavenly Made

Written by Michelle Peterson

Illustrated by Marisa Weyeneth

Heavenly Made

Print ISBN: 978-1-66780-2-978

eBook ISBN: 978-1-66780-2-985

Written by Michelle Peterson.

Illustrated by Marisa Weyeneth.

To the ones who call me mama:

Sydney, Wynn, and Thayer,

I love you more than you will ever know.

Love, your Mama Bird

For my Lil and Eli - you inspire me in all I do.

I'm blessed to be your mama,

and I love you with all my heart!

This mama bird prayed and prayed,
For you, little one, to be heavenly made.

Storms had come,
days went by,

Then a rainbow
finally danced
across the sky.

3

Weeks passed as we prepared for you,
To join our arms and our family, too.

When you looked at us, you stole our hearts,
Now we hold you close, hoping never to part.

Days were fast, the nights were long,
We swaddled you tightly and sang you our song.

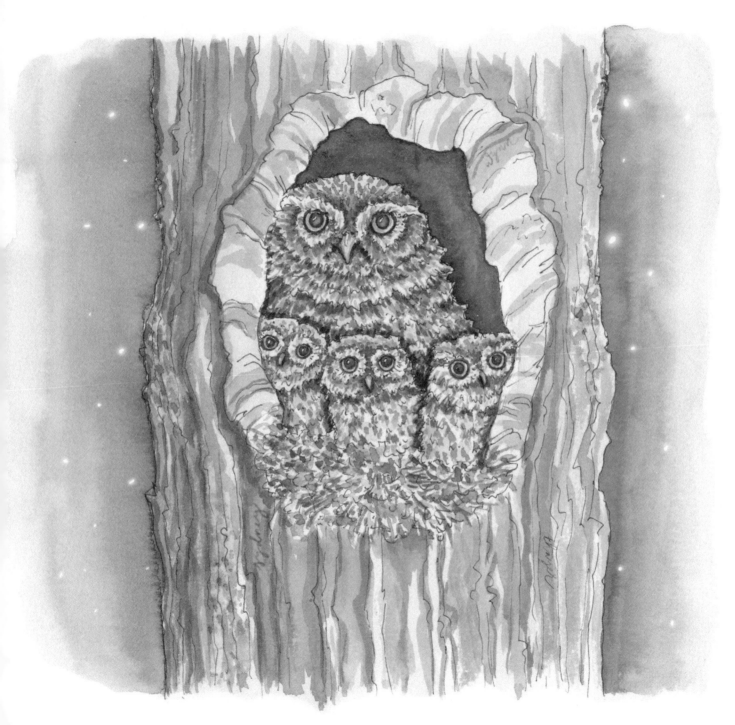

Slow down, dear child, we playfully beg,

As you grow, you smile and stretch your legs.

Adventures, exploring, and creativity peaks,
As we snuggle together, we kiss your cheeks.

We dream you will become independent and strong,
Holding close to the memories of
those days that have gone.

Amazed, proud, and joyous of who you are now,

With the sight of a rainbow,

we think back on our vow.

Joy fills our hearts as we remember the day,
When you, little one, were heavenly made.

ABOUT THE AUTHOR:

MICHELLE PETERSON is the current assistant principal for an elementary school in Morton, Illinois. She has nearly 2 decades of experience in the educational sector in both teaching and administration. Michelle earned a bachelor's degree in Elementary Education from the University of Texas at Austin, as well as, a graduate degree from Bradley University in Educational Leadership. She is currently in an EdD program at Illinois State University. Michelle lives in Morton, Illinois with her husband, and 3 children. This is her first book.

ABOUT THE ILLUSTRATOR:

MARISA WEYENETH is an artist from Metamora, Illinois. Since her childhood, she has had a love for creativity and helping others. This led to her passion for art and education. She pursued both at Eureka College obtaining a Bachelor's degree, and later earned a Master's Degree in Educational Technology. She worked in education for ten years as a teacher then as an Educational Technology Coordinator. During that time, she married the love of her life and had two beautiful children. After starting a family, she pursued art as a creative outlet and has since become a full time artist. Her favorite part of being an artist is the joy her creations bring to others.